REMEMBER WHEN...

REMEMBER WHEN...

Recollections from a Montana Generation Xer

TERRI DRAKE STOLTZ

To order additional copies of this book, contact:
Xlibris Corporation
1-888-795-4274
www.Xlibris.com
Orders@Xlibris.com
81990

This book is dedicated to my wonderful family. To my husband, Steve, thank you for being so patient, understanding, and encouraging. To our children, Colton and Courtney, thank you for allowing us to do our best to raise you correctly, for growing up into wonderful adults, and moving on positively with your own lives. I'm so glad that you both have your own memories from your youth and that you're creating more while living on your own. I decided to fill the void from your absence with something that I have always longed to do, and that was to write. To my parents, David and Kathy; my grandparents; great-grandparents; and everyone in between, thank you all for greatly influencing my life and creating all these precious memories. These recollections are what I remember from my life. Thank you *all* for being there for me!

Contents

Preface

Remember when life seemed much simpler? When we didn't have so much to do in so little time? When life had little or no worries? When we didn't know about or concern ourselves with the world's problems? Well, when I was growing up, that is what I remember. I was born in April of 1965 and was raised in the late '60s, '70s, and the early '80s, classifying me as a first-year Generation Xer. I just missed being a baby boomer by a few months.

Some readers will be the same age as me, born between 1964 and 1965. They will understand and enjoy being taken down memory lane. Others will be older, but most will be younger. Those who were born before 1964 will think that we had it way too easy, and those who are younger, born after the year 1980, will wonder how we ever lived like we did.

The people born before 1945 are called pre-baby boomers. Those born between 1946 to 1964 are called baby boomers, and those born between 1965 to 1979 are called Generation Xers, and the people born between 1979 to 1996 are called the Generation Yers or millennials. Those born after 1996 to my knowledge have yet to be described by a certain title.

When I was growing up, we didn't have answering machines, cell phones, home computers, e-mails, microwave ovens, remotes, and many other things that we have today in the year 2010. So I invite you to please turn the page and enjoy reading about *Remember When*.

Acknowledgments

I would like to give special thanks to my husband, Steve, who has given me support throughout the entire process of writing this book of memories and how different it is today from when we were growing up. I am also grateful to him for giving me our two beautiful children and helping *our* family create its own precious memories. It was when our youngest child moved away after high school that I felt I needed something to do to fill my time. It was Steve who suggested that I write a book since I was always saying that I wanted to.

A big thank-you also goes to Jay Simons for editing this work for me. Without her help, who knows what a big run-on sentence it would read like. She helped me out a lot with her vast knowledge of writing through her adult writing class that she teaches in her free time. It showed me that we are never too old to learn. Thank you!

Lastly, I would like to thank my family as a whole. Without them and their love, this book of "remember whens . . ." wouldn't have been possible.

Note to readers: At the end of each chapter, I've included a couple of blank pages for you to write down your own recollections, memories, and experiences from your life. This will enable you to share them with others, those who might not otherwise know these certain things. I hope you will take advantage of this opportunity to share this information and that you enjoy yourself in the process. Happy remembering!

(1)

Remember When . . .
Communication Was Much Simpler

When I was growing up, if someone wanted to get in touch or talk with someone, they would actually go see that person, or if that was not feasible, they would call them on the telephone from home. Most  homes had a corded rotary dial phone in a lovely shade of green, yellow, tan, or standard black mounted on the wall or sitting on the counter. This is a pink rotary dial phone that had a special silver covering on it. In Medicine Lake,  Montana, where we lived for my teen years—the years when most girls spend a great deal of time on the telephone—the telephone number prefix was 789. It seemed to take forever for the dial to circle around almost the entire way for each number to complete the dialing of the phone number!

You also had to stay in close proximity to the phone because the cord was attached to the phone's receiver. I'm sure that my mom was happy about that since my sister, Devi, and I couldn't say too much without her overhearing our side of the conversation. If a person was lucky, their family's telephone had an extra long cord. Then you wouldn't be stuck in one spot for the entire time you were on the phone.

Later, we were fortunate enough to get a phone that had push buttons. A push-button phone could be set to pulse or tone. Yeah! No more rotary dialing! This was a huge time-saver for those long numbers that some places had. That brings me to another point, most homes only had *one* phone. I also had to ask for permission to use the phone unlike today, where most kids have their own phones. (Cell phones, that is, and  when I say kids, I mean kids. Children as young as ten have their own cell phones. Some may even be younger. I can understand their needing one for emergencies, but just for texting and getting in touch with their friends, come on! Texting is when a person sends a text message on their cell phone to someone else's cell phone. I'm getting ahead of myself though. There will be more regarding cell phones later.)

Long-distance calls were seldom made because these calls were very expensive. Unless there was an emergency or it was a special occasion.

Most homes of those people that lived in the country where there was less population had party lines. The party lines allowed homes in the same area to use the same phone line. Each house on the telephone line had its own distinctive ring. For example, one house's ring would be one long and two short rings. It was easy to eavesdrop with this setup. Most people were honest enough not to listen in. Although sometimes this feature allowed neighbors who wanted to talk to each other to do just that. Just like conference calling today.

When I was a teen, if you were somewhere other than your house and needed to use the telephone, there were phone booths placed strategically throughout the towns and in some businesses. These were square glass booths that had pay phones in them. The door would open and close like a bifold closet door. At first, the phones were rotary dial phones. Later, they were upgraded to push button. When I was a kid, it cost ten cents to make one local phone call. If your call was long distance, you would need to have a couple of dollars in change handy. The operator would come on the line and tell you to put more money in every two minutes if your conversation wasn't finished. It was fun to make a call on a pay phone, unless you ran out of money. But even as a kid, I didn't like using *my* money!

Long-distance calls could be placed through the operator and be charged to the phone line that was being called. These were called collect calls. If you wanted to place a collect call, all that needed to be done was to dial 0 for the operator. When the operator answered, you would tell her that you wanted to place a collect call. She (and I say *she* because most of the telephone operators when I was a kid were women) would ask you your name; then when the party you were calling picked up the telephone and said "hello," the operator would ask if they would pay for a collect call from—. Then you would say your name. After waiting to make sure the call was going to be paid for, the operator would hang up, and you could start your conversation. You had to be quick since they were paying for the charges.

These calls cost more than if the person accepting the collect call just dialed directly themselves. So some people would use this service and not accept the charges. For instance, if you were supposed to call your family out of town after arriving home from a visit and didn't want to pay for a phone call, when the operator asked if you would like to accept the charges, the person on the other line would say no. This way they knew you made it home, and it didn't cost anyone anything.

Today there are still a few pay phones around, although not near as many as when I was growing up. The pay phones are all updated to the push-button kind. It would be interesting to know if there are any rotary dial pay phones still in use.

The corded telephone gave way to the cordless telephone, which was invented in 1965, but only became affordable for the average American family in 1984. By 1994, the demand for these phones greatly increased. The first cordless telephones had antennas that were either stationary or ones that had to be pulled out when there was a call. This allowed for better reception. The cordless telephones of today have built-in antennas, so they aren't so cumbersome.

It is very entertaining to me to be watching a movie or television show and see what style of telephone they are using. A person can tell approximately when the movie or television show was made just by that.

There were no answering machines. The only way to leave a message was to see the person or leave a message on a piece of paper with someone else. I remember taking messages to the neighbors and other people for my mom on my bike. Today, voice messages can be left on a telephone, cell phone, via text on their cell phone, by computer through e-mail, or by using voice mail.

Cell phones have come a long way in a very short time. I remember our first cell phone was a bag phone, purchased in 1992. It was a large rectangular-shaped black bag with a corded telephone the size of a household phone. The reception was pretty good on it though. From there, we graduated to a smaller phone and have tried to keep up with the times by getting smaller phones as they are made. Some of the current cell phones are as flat as a small checkbook and are the size of a small tablet of paper.

It would seem that some of us might be going in the opposite direction, however. Some people have Blackberrys and larger cell phones that do even *more* things. A Blackberry is a wireless handheld device with all the usual PDA (personal digital assistant) applications with a focus on e-mail. Other cell phones today do way more than we need them to in my opinion. They can take pictures, record videos, play music, and also hook up to the Internet to name a few things.

It seems like everyone today has a cell phone, and some homes don't have landlines anymore. They only use their cell phones for all their telephone needs. Therefore, when we call someone today, one of the first questions that we ask is, "Where are you?" instead of "How are you?" This is unfortunate since some areas don't have good coverage and, therefore, lack clear reception all the time, which results in static and a lot of dropped calls. For some the cell phones aren't as reliable as a standard phone line.

I've witnessed on numerous occasions a very comical situation. In a retail store where there are a lot of women shopping, a cell phone rings, and most or all of them will hold up their purse close to their ear to listen to know if it is their phone! The availability of different ringtones has lessened this from happening as often, but it still does. (And I *still* find it quite amusing!)

As a side note, I just found out that in the early '70s, Elvis Presley, of whom I am a huge fan, had a working cell phone in his car. It was in a hard case the size of a carry-on piece of luggage. Inside were the phone and the mechanics of the phone. I saw this first cell phone that Elvis used on television, and it was even bigger than our first cell phone. Apparently, he enjoyed the James Bond movies and all the new gadgets that they used.

The next great invention that stemmed from the telephone was the fax machine, which is short for facsimile or a copy. These are hooked up to a phone line to receive or send documents. They transmit the information through a series of beeps. It was always frustrating to dial a phone number expecting it to ring and have someone answer only to find out that you had dialed a fax number. It didn't take long to realize this since there was a loud startling continuous *beep* on the other end. The first time I used a fax machine I put the document in with the front of the document facing up, not down, and it didn't work. I hope a lot of other people have done this and not just me.

Some pre-baby boomers have just mastered these machines and talk about all the other new inventions, similar to me, in awe, and we reminisce about the earlier days and how much easier things were! There are those from my generation who have mastered some or all the new technology, and I truly admire them. I seem to do only what I have to do to get by.

Computers—the new technology in communication, aren't they wonderful? For most in my generation, computers weren't introduced to us until our late-high school years, if at all. My small class C school, in Medicine Lake, Montana, was able to get a few Apple computers in the spring of 1983, my senior year. My knowledge of computers was very limited during high school. The concept of being able to type and then make changes before you were finished seemed impossible and was mind-boggling to me. I was used to typing on a manual typewriter, which didn't require electricity and were very hard to type on.

Using a manual typewriter requires pushing the keys down very hard in order for the key to strike the ink ribbon and then transfer letters onto the paper. These typewriters had a handle called a return that protruded out of the side. When it was time to go to the next line, it involved reaching up and pushing the return handle, allowing the roller inside to move to rotate the paper up and move the carriage to the beginning of the next line.

It was awful when you made a mistake because you had to use an eraser similar to a pencil eraser. This was especially challenging if you needed more than one copy of your document. Carbon paper was placed between each piece of paper and then you had to correct each page. It was dirty and smudged easily. Not only the copies but your fingers also.

The manual typewriter gave way to the electric typewriter. This new typewriter allowed two choices for the font, pica or elite, and the choice of either single- or double-spacing. The electric typewriter was easier to use, and it improved everyone's typing time, but was much easier to make mistakes on. Some of the new electric typewriters had the capability to use a correction tape. This correction tape would allow a mistake to be typed over with the push of a button and then you could keep typing. Installing one of these into the typewriter was a challenge, but worth it in the end.

The product Wite-Out came along and then correcting mistakes was extremely easy. This would allow a person to correct their mistakes with a small amount of Wite-Out product and then allowing it to dry before retyping correctly. If there were a lot of mistakes, it still didn't look very professional, but if there were only a few mistakes, they were fixed. Today, Wite-Out comes in the liquid or as a tape. Not many people have and still use typewriters, but those who do probably have this product. It comes in handy for other things as well.

What is interesting to me is that when I was in high school, typing was an elective class that most students took so that they could learn how to type and improve their typing skills. Shorthand was also an elective class that was offered. I took both Typing I and II and Shorthand I and II. Today typing and shorthand are not even offered in school. Technology has bypassed the typewriter with the invention of the computer, and there is no need for dictation due to the invention of devices that record voices, making shorthand obsolete. It was fun to pass notes in school written in shorthand though, because even then, most kids couldn't read it.

Students today take "keyboarding" early in their educational years. They start now in grade school to prepare them for their use on computers. Multimedia is offered in some junior high schools and high schools for students to learn how to do even more on computers.

But I digress, I also didn't get any additional experience on computers during my time in college in the early '80s since the college didn't have any computers for the students to use. So I only started using computers when I began working in the real world in 1984 using small business computers, cash registers, and then our own home personal computer, or PC, as they are known today. My first business computer was DOS, or data operating system, for microcomputers. I didn't know *anything* about programming, so if there ever was a problem with the computer, I had to have a computer technician to help me out. Today there is Windows, and it is much more user-friendly, even for someone as computer challenged as myself.

I think computers are wonderful when they work and when a person puts the correct information into them, but sometimes, they crash. Then they aren't so wonderful. When a computer system goes down, it cripples many businesses. When our computer at our place of business was not working, and we had to call a technician, I would get so frustrated when they would end up saying, "Well, just turn it off, wait a few minutes, and then turn it back on." This usually worked; however, we still had to *pay them* for the technical support call. It didn't take us long to just try it ourselves without calling the technician.

Computers also give us another way to keep in touch and that is through electronic mail. E-mail is a handy tool to send people a short note, pictures, or jokes. It seems that when a home finally gets a computer, the e-mailing gets a little out of control with jokes and junk until a person realizes how much time they are spending on them and how silly most are! I know our home did this. Whatever happened to sending a good old-fashioned letter through the post office? Or snail mail as it is sometimes referred to today. I, for one, really take pleasure in receiving a letter from someone or a check payable to me rather than the bills that always come. Someone once told me that the checks payable to yourself are called *bobs*. (Just like the term *bills* that come in the mail is a man's name, these are called *bobs*, which is another common name for some men.) I truly like getting *bobs* instead of *bills*. Paying bills online with a home computer is becoming increasingly popular. This enables the money to be directly taken out of a bank account and paid to the other party electronically, which happens immediately. Who knows how much longer we'll need the post office.

While letter writing has almost become a thing of the past, journaling and noting family history has also become less popular. People really need to take the time and write things down for their family members, now and in the future. It is my hope that whoever is reading this book will take advantage of the space at the end of each chapter for just that purpose.

The Internet is another time waster for me. There is endless information there. Give me the good old days when we had to look stuff up in the encyclopedia. Encyclopedias are large volumes of books containing information on subjects ranging from *A* to *Z*. These were found in the libraries and some homes. Today, there are computer programs and disks that have the encyclopedia information on them, which is always being updated. These are better, but if the computer crashes, there is no backup of this information unless you have a set of encyclopedias on hand. Luckily, most libraries and some schools do.

Google is a search engine that is a very good place to find out information on about most anything. We also have eBay and Craigslist; if a person is looking to buy or sell anything, they can use these tools. I must confess that the Internet can be helpful when looking up airline prices, specials from stores, or other ways to save money; but mostly, I feel it is a way to waste too much time. Especially for those who have addictive personalities, the Internet can be a scary place. A person's time could be spent more productively if they weren't surfing the Internet among other things.

I remember as a kid watching the cartoons *The Flintstones* and *The Jetsons*, what a difference between the two! If you're unfamiliar with these cartoons, *The Flintstones* is about a family and how they live in the prehistoric age. *The Jetsons* is about a family and how they live in the space age. These were on TV about the same time, and I enjoyed watching them both as a kid. How I longed for the days when a person could just push a button and their dinner was ready without having to cook. Or they were dressed without having to pick anything out. Most intriguing to me was the ability to talk on the telephone and actually be able to *see* the other person. (Of course, Mrs. Jetson had a mask that she would put on if she had just gotten out of bed, didn't look her best, or just wasn't quite ready to face anybody.) Can you imagine my amazement when people can actually do that today with the Webcam, the small camera on their computer? Minus the masks, however, as no one has invented something like this yet to my knowledge.

Computer printers have also come a long way in the last few decades. I remember the first printers had rollers with pegs on the sides that would match the perforated paper. The perforated sides with the holes in it would have to be removed when the document was finished printing. The rollers would allow the paper to feed through the printer. This paper would be on one large ream with each page separated by perforation. If you printed a lot of documents or pages, then they would just fold together after they were printed. Separating these pages was called bursting, and it was quite tedious.

Some businesses today such as some banks and financial institutions still have these printers. They must have their reasons; however, I am glad that the computer printers that are in most homes and businesses have the single page without any perforated edges and aren't attached together and need to be separated. This is another time-saver, and the printed pages look much more professional.

The ways to store and save information on computers have drastically changed and greatly improved. Our first computer had floppy disks that were used to save information. These were soft square floppy black disks that were put in the computer and information would be backed up onto it. Next came the disk that was much smaller in size. It was still a square black disk that would be placed into the computer, only it was much smaller, and information would be saved or backed up onto it. Today the most popular ways to save and store information are on a CD, a zip drive, flash drive, or a memory stick. These are all very popular and easy to use since they are simply placed into the correct port on the computer, and the file is saved onto whichever device you're using. Most computers today have the compatibility to use any or all these newer products.

From the PC, technology has advanced to the laptop computer. These are small notebook-sized computers that can do everything that a home computer can except that they are portable. That is what I'm using to type this book, and it *still* amazes me!

A new product has just been invented called the iPad. This is basically a flat-screen laptop computer. As long as you are a subscriber to an Internet carrier, you can use it to connect to the Internet anywhere. Similar to some smart phones today.

Books today can be read on handheld, computer-like devices. There are a couple of brands available now in these eReaders as they are called. There is the Kindle, Nook, and the eBook Reader. Nintendo has joined in and has created the Nintendo DS that allows a person to read up to one hundred books that it has stored in it. These devices come in handy for people traveling due to their size and the number of books that they hold. Again, I find myself liking the old way of reading a book. Maybe one day I might change, but not at this time of my life.

The PalmPilot is another item that some people really love; it is a handheld device that enables someone to put in information such as their schedule and important things to remember. I am still writing these things down on paper and on my calendar. It is very hard for me to change.

The computer age has also brought with it the ability to network through social networking sites (SNS). These Web-based social networking spaces make it possible for individuals or groups of people to create a profile of themselves, and then, they can share that profile with members of the same social networking space. Today there are many SNS to choose from: Facebook, MySpace, Twitter, and LinkedIn are among some of the more popular ones.

Communicating on these networking sites has become increasingly popular with a huge number of people. Besides reading what is on a specific person's profile, you can instant message them, spend time in a chat room, and send them an e-mail or site mail, watch videos, and so on. This is a great way to find people and catch up on what is happening in their lives.

With every new thing, however, it seems that some people have to ruin it. This seems to be the case with these networking sites. There are those who are bullying others. The term for this is called cyberbullying. It's hard enough to be a teenager with all its emotional ups and downs. Bullying, without the use of computers and the networking sites, is sometimes included in these downs unfortunately. Now I can't believe that some people are using these networking sites to *add* to the bullying that is already being done. There are even some teenagers who have committed suicide due to the cyberbullying that has been done to them.

All these networking sites are way too technologically challenging for me. However, the kids of the next generation, the Generation Yers, all really love them. Give me the good old days any day.

After a long day at work, school, or home, it just seems to take so much extra time to do the other necessary things to finish your day. Looking through your mail (snail mail, that is), checking your telephone messages on your answering machine, listening to your voice mail on your cell phone, reading your e-mails, *and* then completing your day or evening by now. What happened to these technological advances in communication helping us to *save* time?

My Own Recollections

(2)

Remember When . . .
Cooking Meant Actually Cooking

When I was a kid, there were no such things as fast-food restaurants and prepackaged foods. Fast food was nonexistent until McDonald's opened. There was only one McDonald's in Billings, Montana, the largest town in our state at this time. Today, there seems to be a McDonald's every few miles, along with all the other restaurant chains. Could this be one of the reasons for the epidemic of overweight and obese people in the United States? When we did go to McDonald's for a meal, it was a really big treat. So of course, it didn't happen very often.

The first big-box store, a term used to describe a style of physically large chain stores also called superstore, megastore, or supercenter, that came to Billings, Montana, was at or about the same time as McDonald's. This store was Kmart. The Kmart that opened in our town had a café in it, similar to a deli, but it was cafeteria style. It was so much fun to get to go shopping for school clothes or shoes and also get a meal. Or better yet, a treat after our shopping was done. I really enjoyed sitting there after shopping and listening to my mom visit with her friends or our relatives that were there with us. When I was older and was able to go to the café with my sister or a friend while Mom shopped, well, that was even *more* fun. It made me feel so grown-up.

Eventually more big-box stores opened, and the café in Kmart closed. They probably did this so they could use the floor space for inventory that would sell and ultimately make more money for the store. Today the box stores all have some sort of food court or fast-food restaurant chain in them.

The reason there were no prepackaged foods was that the microwave oven wasn't invented yet. Everything needed to be cooked and/or warmed up on the stove or in the oven. A few people had toaster ovens. These are small metal boxes similar to a regular oven that sit on the kitchen counter. They have the ability to toast bread and whatever else you might want toasted or heated up.

The first prepackaged foods that I remember are the frozen TV dinners that were purchased from the grocery store. These came in aluminum trays that had separate compartments for the different foods. They had meat, potatoes, gravy, a vegetable, and a dessert (the all-American meal). These were so cool! We baked them in the oven and ate them on our TV trays while watching TV. My two favorite pastimes are eating and watching TV. These dinners were not the best tasting and probably not very healthy. The meat was usually hard and dry, the potatoes seemed to always get crusty around the edges, and the dessert was likely to burn, but it was so much fun to get to actually eat in the living room while watching television. As with most things that are new and convenient, these cost more than food that needed to be prepared and cooked, so my family didn't get to eat these very often. When we did though, I loved it. It felt like a very special time to me.

I remember, while living in Billings, Montana, during my earlier school years, we had milk and other dairy products delivered to us at our home. Weekly, the milkman would come early in the morning and place our order in the square insulated metal milk box. This kept the dairy products from getting too warm and spoiling. I thought this was how everyone got milk. When we moved from the city of Billings to a smaller town, Medicine Lake, Montana, I realized that you could also buy milk in the grocery store. What a wonderful convenience though to have it delivered every week and not have to worry about it.

School lunch has changed since I was in school too. When I was in grade school, I took a lunch every day that my mom had packed for me. I remember it usually being mainly a sandwich or soup in a thermos along with a dessert of some kind. Sometimes I was lucky enough to have a Snack Pack pudding in my lunchbox. This was usually eaten first, and I *always* had to lick the lid off. The containers that the pudding came in were metal. The lid was also metal, and the edges were rather sharp. I was always told not to lick the pudding off the lid, but that didn't stop me from doing it; and no matter how careful I was, I sometimes cut my tongue. It pretty much ruined the taste of the pudding for a while, but I never seemed to learn my lesson from this. I guess I didn't want to waste the pudding that was always on the lid. Today these containers and lids are made out of plastic. So no matter if we lick the lids off, we won't cut our tongues.

In junior high school and high school, we were offered school lunch through a hot-lunch program. This allowed students to purchase their lunches and not bring a lunch from home. It seems that today taking a lunch to school isn't cool, so not many students do this. Some kids nowadays don't even take the time to eat lunch at all. They spend this free time doing other things, which makes no sense to me at all. Some schools these days even offer breakfast for the students. It is a shame that not more kids take advantage of the good wholesome food that is prepared for them.

Now schools have vending machines for the students and teachers to purchase all kinds of things. Some sell soda pop, juice, and water, while others sell snacks of all kinds. This enables the schools to make a little extra money, but it is at the expense of our kids' health. Some parents' organizations and groups have boycotted the vending machines in schools. A few states have listened and either removed the machines or have only allowed healthy items to be placed in them, which I think is a benefit to our kids' health, since most don't eat lunch at school and will choose instead to purchase something that isn't full of harmful ingredients. The very best solution would be to remove all the vending machines entirely and then maybe the kids would eat the lunches at their schools.

There were no fancy kitchen gadgets to cook in either while I was growing up. We didn't have George Foreman Grills, Air Pop Popcorn Machines, or any other special things to make cooking easier and/or faster.

Soda pop came in bottles. When the aluminum can came along, they had pull tabs on top that a person would just peel off and discard, under which was an opening for the person to drink from. The cans were then made with the tab attached, and it just pierced a hole in the top as they are today. There are also the plastic bottles available now along with the aluminum cans.

Recycling has become a big thing in the country to help with all the garbage and waste that we now produce. I always enjoyed going to the recycling center and turning our cans into money. It always seemed like we got *a lot* of money for our cans; however, I'm sure that is because I didn't know how much things actually cost. It was always neat to watch the cans being emptied into the big container and then being weighed. I liked the feeling I got when we would recycle our cans, and I still do. It means less garbage filling up our landfills. Many people recycle both the aluminum cans and the plastic bottles that soda pop comes in today. Even in some cities and towns, recycling glass, paper, and cardboard is mandatory.

Coffee was made by percolating coffee grounds in a pot on the stove. Today we have automatic-drip coffeepots. Some of these coffeemakers even have timers on them so that the coffee is already brewed when a person wakes up. Some people like to grind their own coffee beans, and they can do this with the convenience of a small grinder in their kitchen. There are the espresso machines that allow us to have lattes, mochas, breves, and more. Today it is actually hard to get just a regular cup of plain coffee unless you're at a restaurant.

Ice cube trays used to be metal with a handle attached that would need to be pulled up to release the ice. Today there are plastic ice cube trays that just twist and the ice comes loose from the edge of the tray. Many people have automatic ice makers in their refrigerators, and the ice just falls into a large bin in the freezer when it is ready. The ice maker shuts off automatically when the bin is full.

Bread machines were a wonderful invention for me. We purchased one around 1987, and it was the first time I had ever made a loaf of bread from scratch. These machines have the capability to hold all the ingredients to make a loaf of bread, mix the ingredients, knead the dough, allow the bread dough to rise at just the right temperature, then knead the dough again, allow it to rise again, and then bake the dough into a perfect loaf of bread. What a wonderful alternative to thawing and baking the frozen bread dough that was available in the grocery store or by doing it all by hand.

This first bread machine of ours was shaped like R2-D2 in Star Wars. The first few times that we used the bread machine everything went great. There *was* one time I remember using it, and while putting the ingredients into the machine, thinking that I had forgotten something, I pulled the pan out from the machine. This enabled some of the wet ingredients to seep into the area where there shouldn't have been anything other than the chamber for the inside of the machine. I quickly pushed it back in place and continued with the process. The bread baked, and I took it out. My family and I ate the bread, and I thought everything was great. However, when I went to clean the machine, the inside wouldn't come out. It had baked itself together! Try as hard as we could, my husband and I couldn't get it apart. Even when we had a visit from my dad, he and my husband couldn't get it apart. The bread machine was still under warranty for a short time, and I'm embarrassed to say that we sent it back for a replacement. Boy, did I ever learn my lesson not to pull out the pan after starting a loaf of bread.

Over the years, they have improved how they make the bread machines, and now, the inside is a completely separate closed unit. The paddle is located inside the pan and not in the chamber. The ingredients are still placed inside the pan and then the pan goes inside the machine. This really made it even more convenient. I'm wondering if the bread machine companies had a lot of returns on those first ones from people like me. We have gone through several bread machines and have enjoyed using them, although there is still one problem. We eat *way* more bread than we need.

Popcorn was made on the stove in a kettle, or if you were lucky, you bought Jiffy Pop Popcorn. This was a product that had the uncooked corn kernels and other ingredients in the inside of a big round foil container. It had a handle on it, and when placed on the stove, the foil would expand as the kernels of corn popped. When it was finished popping, there would be a big mound of popped corn inside the foil. Inevitably, I would become impatient when opening the foil, and a burst of steam would come out, which sometimes burned my hands or forearms.

This was followed by the invention of air-popped popcorn machines. These were wonderful since they allowed the popcorn to pop in record time without the oil that was necessary when popping corn on the stove. Making popcorn this way is healthier unless you add butter when it is done. This machine also saved a lot of time in the process of making popcorn.

I remember a few times that the top wasn't on properly on our air popper and the popcorn was just popping right out of the machine. Popcorn was everywhere. About the same time as the air popper was introduced, microwave popcorn was available for purchase in the stores. They came in paper bags that allowed the popcorn to pop inside along with the oil and flavorings. These were very handy for a quick snack without the mess. Some even tasted as good as the popcorn available at the movie theaters. However, sometimes the popcorn would cook faster and burn. People had to figure out how much time was the best amount of time to pop the microwave popcorn in their microwave. The usual time was anywhere between three to five minutes.

A favorite treat was to purchase a box of Cracker Jacks. These were boxes of caramel-covered popcorn with peanuts. The best part of buying this treat was the special toy inside. When I was a kid, the boxes of Cracker Jacks were bigger, and the toys were actually toys that could be played with. It seems that today the boxes are much smaller, and the toys are only stickers and other little things like that.

George Foreman Grills and similar products are another great invention that helped people eat healthier while saving time. These are small kitchen appliances that cook boneless meat in a very short time without any need for oil. They have nonstick surfaces in the lid and on the bottom of them that both heat up and cook the meat faster since there is no need to flip the meat and cook both sides. The meat is cooked very similar to being grilled on the barbecue, but only, it is in your house. This is perfect for the winter when the weather in Montana is too cold to barbecue outside.

Dishwashers were very different back when I was a kid also. Instead of being built-in, they started out as a big unit that you rolled over to the sink, attached the hose from the dishwasher to the faucet in the kitchen, and then turned on the hot-water spigot. When it was time for the dishwasher to drain and then rinse, the water would come out of the bottom of that same hose into the sink and down the drain. When the cycle was finished, the dishwasher was simply unhooked and rolled back to wherever it was stored when not in use. The top of the dishwasher usually had a wood surface that could be used as a cutting board. I suppose this also created another surface to work on. We never had a dishwasher in our home when I was growing up. My grandmother and aunt did though, and it was *always* more fun to do the dishes there.

Some other kitchen conveniences that have improved our lives are the electric can opener and the electric knife. (Can you imagine having to use something manually?) Granted, today I don't use an electric knife that often, but when I do, it sure is nice. The electric knife works beautifully when a nice loaf of homemade bread needs slicing!

The electric can openers today are wonderful; some are so small that you don't even see them on the kitchen counter. Some are located under the cabinet, so they aren't even on the kitchen counter, and others today cut the lid off *without* leaving a rough edge. The electric can openers from my childhood were either brown, gold, or yellow and were very cumbersome. The can would catch on a magnet and then you would push down on the top. This would make the can go around until the lid was cut off from the can. I was always somewhat afraid that the can would slip off and fall, or I would somehow cut myself on the edge of the can or on the lid.

When I was growing up and even in my early adult life, *buying* water to drink was unthinkable. I didn't like the idea of spending money on bottled water, so I invested in a good water purifier and carried my own reusable container to hold my drinking water in. This way I didn't have to purchase my water *and* throw away all that plastic.

The bottled water industry makes a lot of money today, even though it isn't good for the environment with the disposal of all the plastic bottles. If people choose to purchase water, I would hope that they would at least buy it in larger containers and not buy all those small plastic bottles since they just end up in our Dumpsters and landfills. There are some people who do recycle and I commend them for it; however, there are a lot of reusable bottles on the market today that can be purchased instead of continuing to buy the plastic bottles that get thrown away after one use.

My Own Recollections

(3)

Remember When . . .
Family Seemed Closer

Remember when family seemed closer *both* in their relationships *and* distance? When I was growing up, I remember that most of our extended family lived close together, at least in the same state or the state next to us. It was easier for us to get together. Today, it appears that most young adults move away and, more often than not, out of the state they grew up in to make their mark in the world. This seems to be true especially in Montana, where it appears there aren't a lot of areas of opportunity for young adults to pursue professional careers, at least for a competitive wage and a good retirement program.

A generation ago, and even two generations ago, our parents and grandparents earned a decent wage to raise a family. They were able to buy a house and support their family. These simple things are getting harder and harder to do for the next generation. Today, many families are overextended in credit, which leads to a huge number of people in great debt. A saying that I recently heard says it all, and I, for one, am taking it to heart: "Use it up, wear it out, make it do, or do without!"

I have heard numerous times from people ranging in age from their midforties up to fifty-five and even some people that are older say that they are not going to retire and live where they are currently living. They want to move back to a town and/or state that isn't so populated and fast paced, like Montana. I can't blame them. I am so happy that I was able to be raised in a small town in Montana and then to raise *my* family in a small town in Montana. Staying in Montana has given me and my family a happy, peaceful, and less-stressful life. It appears as though we trade in the wonderful retirement plan for our futures for a better way of life now.

When I was growing up, families were closer also in their relationships. My family spent evenings together. We would always have supper, we would clean up the kitchen, and then we would usually watch TV where the programming was much more family oriented than it is today. (More on that later.) Unfortunately, we started to have less of this family time when my sister and I were in high school. But fortunately, we had experienced our family time during our most vulnerable years.

I remember having nicknames thought up by my sister and me with a little help from our dad. One evening my dad said to my sister, "You're goofy!" I immediately thought that I needed a nickname too, so I asked my dad what my nickname was. He thought quickly and said, "You're Nuts!" We gave Dad the nickname Handsome. We knew we couldn't leave anyone out, so we asked what Mom's nickname was. He replied that hers was Pretty. The nicknaming wasn't complete until we had one for our dog. He was a cocker spaniel that was named Corky. We gave him the nickname Hairy. The nicknames never really stuck, but we did enjoy telling our friends and family what they were.

Some evenings we would play board games. Monopoly was a family favorite. I loved it because it was a *very* long game, and that meant we would play for at least a couple of hours. Other board games that we played were Clue, Sorry, and Aggravation. Our grandpa made us a wooden board that the game Don't Get Mad was played on. The pattern for this game came from a family member who had seen it being played in Italy. This game is similar to the game of Aggravation, but with slightly different rules. We also played a lot of card games.

Weekends were spent with family and friends. Our family would regularly go visit other families. The adults would play cards while the children would play outside and then eventually fall asleep on the floor. It was usually a wonderful time, and I really enjoyed being carried from the car into the house by Dad. However, it wasn't as special when I was bigger, and my parents had to wake me up, and I had to *walk* in by myself.

I remember my dad taking me and my sister along sometimes in the eighteen-wheeler he was driving at the time for a living. We talked on the CB radio, a citizens band radio. This is a system of short-distance radio communications between people on a selection of forty channels. These could be used without needing to get a license. He taught us how to use the CB language for talking on the CB. It was a lot of fun to talk to the men driving the other trucks. We even had our own handles or names while talking on the CB. We would also sit in the sleeper of the cab and rest our heads on the back  of the truck and then say, "Ahhhhh . . ." This would allow our heads to bounce on and off the back of the truck. Why we thought this was fun, I have no idea, but we did. I'm sure this was very annoying to our dad, but he never got mad or told us to stop.

When my dad was driving truck, he drove Mack trucks. He was partial to these, so when he purchased a Toyota pickup truck, he had a tailgate made especially for it. It read, "When I grow up, I want to be a Mack truck." It really was cute and very clever.

Another very cool invention for the automobiles and trucks was the radar detector or fuzz buster as it was called. These were a fascinating new phenomenon of the time since it allowed drivers to be aware when a policeman or highway patrolman had his radar gun on your vehicle to check to see if you were speeding. These were plugged into the cigarette lighter and usually sat on the front dash of the vehicle. They would beep when it detected the radar, thus eliminating a lot of speeding tickets. They would detect other things also, so there were a few false alarms on some of our travels. Today we have GPS, a global positioning system, which uses satellites and measurements that are displayed to the user that helps us with locations on a map, thus helping us get from place to place.

Our family took weekend trips a lot. We lived about ninety miles from the town of Fort Smith, Montana. The Big Horn River was located near Fort Smith and a dam, the Yellowtail Dam, was built there, which created the Big Horn Lake. My dad loved to fish, boat, and camp, so this was an ideal location for our family weekend trips. We would camp in the campground by the After Bay near the dam. We would launch the boat in the After Bay or up at the lake. Dad would let all of us kids—my sister, all our cousins that were with us on the boat, and I—steer the boat. We all loved doing that and didn't want our turn to end. My dad's brother, my uncle Melvin, and his family lived in Fort Smith, which was a bonus for us all. We went to this lake at least every other weekend in the summer. The most memorable times were when more than just our immediate family was there. These trips were fun, simple, and inexpensive unless the boat had problems.

I went fishing with my dad quite a bit and usually caught fish. I didn't like touching the worms or the fish, so Dad had to always bait the hook for me *and* take the fish off the hook. Looking back, I think I liked spending time with my dad and *not* the fishing. My mom would fillet the fish that we caught and cook them. I don't like the *taste* of fish because I had to eat so much of it as a kid.

In the summertime, my sister and I would be busy with activities. We took tennis lessons, dance lessons, and whatever else was offered in our neighborhood. We rode our bikes and the city bus to the public swimming pool for lessons and also just to swim for fun.

Summers were spent with extended family also. We had family reunions often. We would see cousins, aunts, and uncles that we hadn't seen for quite a while. We all played outdoor games, especially horseshoes. The grownups played in teams of two and then would challenge the others. The kids had watermelon-eating contests among other things. I remember once my sister and I were in one of these contests and my sister won. She won by spitting out more than just the seeds though. The location of the family reunion was the same most of the time too. Family reunions aren't as easy to plan and have as they used to be. Family members live too far away from each other to get together for a family weekend, and most are just too busy.

Devi and I would spend weeklong visits in the summer with our grandparents. Once we took the train with a relative from Billings, Montana, where we lived to our grandparents' house in Glendive, Montana. Passenger trains were more popular in those days for travel. There were different cars  for eating, smoking, or sleeping. Our relative smoked, so we would stay in our seats while he went to the smoking car. Of course, we would get bored, so we would go looking for him. This meant going from car to car. Exciting *and* scary at the same time since between the cars is only a small landing separating *you*

from the *ground*! What an adventure for us. This is what the train station in Glendive, Montana, looks like today.

A few years later when we lived in Medicine Lake, Montana, we would take the small bus by ourselves back and forth. This bus wasn't your typical bus; it wasn't a Greyhound or anything close to it. It was similar to a station wagon car with three rows of bench seats for the driver and the passengers. Most of the time, we would be the *only* passengers. Medicine Lake and Glendive, Montana, weren't popular destinations for too many people.

Our mom's parents lived in Glendive, Montana, in town, which we were used to, so it was a lot like our time spent at home, except that we didn't have chores to do. If we *did* help with the yard work or something else, it didn't *feel* like work. We would stay up late and watch TV with our grandparents. It always felt like we were getting away with something because at home we weren't allowed to stay up past ten o'clock very often. I fell asleep pretty quickly after the prime-time programming was over.

Our mom's sister, our aunt Sandi, lived in Glendive too, and we would spend time with our cousins. They were a few years younger than us, but for the most part, we tried to include them in what we did.

We walked to the public swimming pool to swim, walked downtown, and played with the neighbors. On Sundays, we went to church with Grandma. That was always a very special time for me. We walked to and from church and then had the rest of the day to sit around with Grandma and Grandpa.

Sometimes we went to visit other family members and to pick chokecherries, play games, or just enjoy each other's company. On some of these visiting days, my sister and I would become bored. If we were visiting family that lived in town, we walked back to our grandparent's house. If we were on the south side of Glendive, we had to walk through a tunnel that went under the railroad tracks and this brought us out to the north side of town. This tunnel was a lot of fun to go through. While inside, it would be a great deal cooler than outside in the baking sun. When we made it through the tunnel, it was only a short distance to our destination, a big wonderfully cool house with a yard that provided shade by big crab apple trees. These trees made a mess in the yard, and I remember Grandpa always cussing that poor tree. I liked it because it gave us really good apples that Grandma and Mom would use to make *the best* apple pies.

Today, the tunnel has been updated with a few changes. Lights have been added that come on automatically at dusk and dawn. They have also added a dome to it and paved the pathway, which was gravel when we used it. The picture is what it currently looks like.

On a number of days, we would walk downtown by ourselves and shop at the dime store—Woolworth's. This was always enjoyable since we could sit at the soda fountain, which was along the right wall, and order treats. This dime store was so much fun to shop in. It seemed to have everything that anyone would want. We would buy small toys to play with while on our vacation. Some things did only cost ten cents; today it is hard to find anything that is only ten cents!

Our dad's parents lived in Wibaux, Montana, on a farm along a red dirt road, which we weren't used to, but we truly enjoyed it. This red

dirt road had two spots in it where if the car was going just the right speed, it felt like your stomach was doing a flip. Devi and I got a kick out of that. We would always say to Dad when we got close to those spots, "Go faster, Dad!" Our dad's sister, our aunt Diane, lived down the road on the next farm. I loved spending time outside with Grandpa, visiting with Grandma, and spending time with our cousins. Our cousins were around the same ages as my sister and me, so we had a lot in common. They would take us horseback riding, to town to go to the swimming pool and to the Tasty Hut, which is similar to a Dairy Queen today. This was a time to hang out with other kids that were around at the time. Some were older than we were, and others were younger. We would go there and listen to the jukebox while playing games. They had a foosball

table and pinball machines. I would always try to show off in front of the boys, hoping that they would notice me. Here is a picture of the Tasty Hut as it looks today.

My grandparents' car had a bobblehead dog that sat in the back window. It was so much fun to watch it when the car would hit a bump in the road. The head would move around and make it look like a real dog. Once while riding in their car, Grandpa saw a rattlesnake in the road. He ran it over. Then he backed the car up, got out, and checked to make sure the snake was dead. Unfortunately, my car window was down, and unbeknownst to me, he had cut the rattle off the snake; and on his way back to car, he rattled it right in *my window*! That little incident probably scared at least two years off my life. To this day, I really don't like snakes. I have no idea if this is the reason, but I can only think that it didn't help.

Grandpa took us for rides in his yellow 1959 American Jeep. Some of these were really wild rides. Once, he was driving through the pasture rather fast, and we were heading straight for a big pile of hay. He asked all of us nonchalantly, "Well, what do you think? Should we drive over it?" At this point I was scared to death and screamed, "No!" while my sister and cousins were just laughing and playing along while saying yes! This Jeep was used for spinning brodies in the hay fields and pastures by

Grandpa with us as passengers. If my grandma only knew, she probably wouldn't have let us go for rides in the Jeep. We always wanted to drive but, of course, weren't nearly old enough.

Sometimes we would help Grandpa pick up hay bales. I didn't really enjoy this since we never had the right clothing on, and I got dirty and scratched up. Something that *was* really fun was helping to feed the bum

lambs. This is what the windbreak on the property looks like today and the sheep barn where they kept them along with a couple of pictures of some sheep in the pasture. We would use bottles that looked just like baby bottles but were much larger. I also really enjoyed the baby chicks when they had some. It was so much fun to watch them and listen to them cheep.

If we visited at just the right time, during the summer, it would be branding time. There would be brandings happening at my grandparents' friends on neighboring farms and ranches. These were always fun for me because I could watch the cute cowboys that were around my age, although there were other parts of the brandings that were not so enjoyable. The smell of burnt or singed hair was one and when they took off the horns on some of the cows. This looked incredibly painful and not very humane since they didn't use anything to numb the area first.

There was an old bunkhouse next to the house where my grandparents lived, and I especially enjoyed spending time in there just exploring. When I walked in, I tried to imagine who had been there before me.

It was always musty smelling and quite cool in the summers, *even* in August. There were still pieces of furniture and kitchen things in the bunkhouse. Everything was old and unfamiliar to me—like the wood cookstove in the kitchen. So to me it was fun to look around. In the attic, there were more things to look through. I truly enjoyed playing in the bunkhouse. It has since been torn down, but it was a great place for me to idle away some time when I was a kid.

If we weren't having a family reunion or away at either of our grandparents' houses, we would take vacations together. I remember visiting family a lot. Holidays were spent with grandparents, aunts, uncles, and cousins, anyone who could come. We usually spent each holiday with both sides of our family. Fortunately for us, they lived in towns only thirty miles from each other.

On all these trips, we played games to pass the time. Our favorite seemed to be the Alphabet Game. I'm sure there are many variations on this game, but our version seemed to keep us busy for at least a hundred miles or more. We would have to find words on the highway signs that started with the letter *A* and go all the way through the alphabet to the letter *Z*. My sister usually won, given that she could see the sign way before me and being older gave her an advantage. The letter *Q* was always a tough one to find, followed by *Z*.

We also played the license plate game. This game involved finding as many different license plates that were from other states as possible as you either passed a car or they passed you. This game was much easier to play when traveling on the interstate instead of on the two-lane highways since there wasn't as much traffic.

We sang songs as well. We sang to my dad's favorite song "Sixteen Tons" by Tennessee Ernie Ford. Most times *I* sang songs, and my poor family had to endure *my* singing. My favorites included "America the Beautiful" and "This Land Is Your Land." The "Star-Spangled Banner" was a song I loved to sing too. (These songs were songs I learned in school by the way. In school, we also said the Pledge of Allegiance before starting our school day. Patriotism seems to be lacking in America today, and I find that very distressing.)

One highway sign that I questioned Dad about on one of our trips was the yellow diamond-shaped warning sign that had the words "WATCH FOR

FALLEN ROCK." My dad told me an elaborate story about an Indian maiden who had run away. Her name was Fallen Rock, and we all needed to be on the lookout for her. Every time I would see this sign, I thought about this poor girl and felt sorry for her. I don't know if I saw the other sign for this warning where there was a picture of rocks falling from an edge along with the words or if I actually figured it out.

Stopping for gas was much different during this time too. The gas stations were called filling stations, and they were full service. So when it was time to fill up the car with gas, the gas station attendant did it for you. He usually washed the car windows *and* checked the oil if you asked him to. This is the gas station in Wibaux, Montana, presently. At one point, it was a full-service filling station. Over time, these full-service  gas stations, as they were referred to, changed to *half* full-service and *half* self-service. This allowed people to choose if they wanted all the extra service for more money of course. It seems that today there aren't too many full-service gas stations around. If the bathrooms had outdoor entrances, they weren't locked like they are today. Now a person doesn't even have to enter the building unless they want to purchase something other than gas since they can just pay at the pump with their credit or debit cards.

On these car trips, we didn't travel in luxury either. There was no air-conditioning other than the four windows being rolled down. This meant arriving at your destination very windblown and hot. When my family did have a car with air-conditioning, we didn't use it because we were told it used too much gas. When we *were* going to use it, it was usually not working. I didn't mind too much since I either fell asleep or laid down to pass the time and miles. It certainly seemed like we got to our destination a lot faster when I slept.

As a side note, none of our family cars we had while I was growing up had seat belts. When we did get a car that had seat belts, we never used them. They were usually tucked down in the seat. This was before it was illegal not to wear them. Car seats for babies, infants, and toddlers weren't even invented. Our only protection was our mother's arm reaching over to stop us from hitting the dash. We even rode in the *back* of pickup trucks unattended. I know my parents both didn't enjoy the questions that my sister and I would occasionally ask, "How many more miles?" or "Are we there yet?" We learned at a pretty young age that those questions shouldn't be overused.

My sister and I would usually get pretty rambunctious in the car after a while, and I remember we would draw an imaginary line down the middle of the backseat. If she would go over that line or vice versa, we would be able to hit the other. Not very loving, I know. If *only* we would have had a portable device to watch movies on that are available now!

Various smells bring back several of these wonderful memories for me. Some of them include dust from dirt roads, sagebrush, flowering weeds, fresh-cut hay, Russian olive trees, and particular flowers like the tiger lily and the wild roses.

Certain sights seem to bring back a number of these memories for me too. Such as seeing the wheat fields swaying and rippling in the ever-present northeastern Montana winds along with seeing the hay fields with rows and rows of hay bales.

I remember one of the last trips or drives that I took with my dad as an adult was on the back roads from Glendive, Montana, to Wibaux, Montana. We were going to have lunch with Aunt Diane since we were in

town visiting. On this drive it was Dad, my son, Colton who was about eight or nine years old, and me. Dad showed us the badlands where he used to watch the sheep in the summer and told us who lived where along the way. Even though I was hot, carsick, and hungry, I am *so* grateful that I took the time for that drive and was with him *and* my son on this outing. It will always be a very special memory for me. My dad didn't live for many more years after that memorable summer. My advice to all who are reading these words is to take the time to slow down and spend *quality* time with your loved ones. As sometimes they aren't with us as long as we'd like.

My Own Recollections

(4)

Remember When . . .
Illegal Drugs Meant Pot

While I was growing up, there weren't too many illegal drugs that the average teenager used other than marijuana and possibly cocaine. Of course, there were some individuals that *did* use other drugs, but this was not the norm for most teenagers.

Today there are many more illegal drugs, with meth being the worst and most addicting. This drug is also easily manufactured. Many people do manufacture this drug even though it is extremely dangerous *and* toxic to breathe in the chemicals that are used in the process. They say you never see an old meth addict.

Prescription drugs are also becoming a big problem in the United States. Some people are abusing them, especially the strong painkillers. These prescription painkillers are among some of the prescription drugs that are being sold to other people for a profit.

Marijuana is now legal in some states for those who have a medical marijuana card. This enables the carrier of the card to be able to purchase marijuana from a caregiver for the management of their pain. I can understand that most people with these cards actually do need it for pain control. Yet I am sure that a lot of other people abuse this system and just smoke the marijuana for pleasure. Or they share it with people not needing it for pain control. It is a shame too as the people who *do* need it may lose the right in the future to be able to purchase it legally.

It is almost impossible to get hired for a new job until you pass a drug test today. Some very important positions or jobs even have random drug testing. What does that tell us about our society today?

And
Remember When . . .
Promiscuity Meant Possible Pregnancy

Remember when having premarital sex meant the possibility of getting pregnant? A person could also get a sexually transmitted disease; however, most were treatable, like gonorrhea, with the exception of herpes simplex virus, HSV-1 and HSV-2, viruses that cause infections in humans and produce lifelong infections.

Today, sexual activity leads potentially to many more life-changing effects. Many teenagers today face more grave consequences than we did as teenagers. There is still the risk of pregnancy and sexually transmitted diseases such as herpes, but there is also the issue of potentially contracting HIV (human immunodeficiency virus), AIDS (acquired immune deficiency syndrome), and many more diseases that are life threatening. Is premarital sex worth it? That is a very important question worth asking yourself before engaging in this act.

This might be a good place to discuss the changes in fashion. I can't even begin to describe all the fads and fashion changes that have occurred through the years (that's a whole book in itself), but I believe that our changing society is affecting how each generation looks at the opposite sex *and* their relationships. As time goes by, the clothes get tighter and shorter, and this ultimately shows more of the human body. This all seems to be acceptable in our culture today. It would be nice if modesty came back, even if only a little bit.

Also, the fads seem to come around every twenty years or so, only they adapt to the current lengths. The young people of today are advertising what they can offer the opposite sex by showing so much of their bodies. Leaving a little to the imagination is something we should attain to in our current clothing styles.

And
Remember When . . .
Diseases Were Kept in Check

I remember, while growing up, we were immunized against every known disease in school or at local schools before the school year started. Some of these diseases that we were immunized against were smallpox, polio, mumps, measles, and rubella.

Now it seems that there is a number of other diseases and potential life-threatening viruses that we didn't have to worry about while I was growing up. Such as HIV, AIDS, SARS (severe acute respiratory syndrome), MRSA (methicillin-resistant *Staphylococcus aureus*), hantavirus, West Nile virus, bird flu, H1N1 (a subtype of the species influenza A virus, or better known as the swine flu), and hepatitis—to name a few.

These days we all are aware of the threat of anthrax, the threat of a nuclear attack, WMD (weapons of mass destruction), and any number of terrorist attacks. There seems to be concerns of any number of pandemics that could happen today.

My Own Recollections

(5)

Remember When . . .
Entertainment Was Family Oriented

I remember, while growing up, entertainment was family oriented. TV shows, movies, and music were entertaining. Television shows and programs were made for families. A favorite show of our family's was *The Andy Griffith Show*. This was a show about a father, who is the town sheriff, raising his son with the help of his aunt. They lived in a small fictional town in the south called Mayberry, North Carolina. In each episode, they showed how life situations could be solved with love, quality family values, and humor. My dad really got a kick out of Barney who was the deputy of this town. Barney always seemed to be having an issue about something, and he was very funny to watch. I think I enjoyed seeing and hearing my dad laugh at Barney more than I enjoyed the show. Today the reruns bring all the memories back, and I love to watch them on TV Land.

Happy Days was another show that was on about this same time too. This was about an average family, the Cunninghams, that lived in Milwaukee, Wisconsin, the heart of middle-class America. They had two sons and one daughter, and the premise of the show was focused on how they lived in the 1950s and early 1960s, complete with all the family issues that we all go through, including siblings and friends. My parents both were teenagers during the 1950s, and they could relate to this show quite readily. I found it interesting to watch it and see how things were for them as teenagers. There was no bad language or sex scenes other than the occasional making-out scenes, which was just kissing. When these *would* be on, I was very embarrassed to be watching it with my parents.

Another one of our family's favorite shows to watch together was *Little House on the Prairie*. This featured a family that lived on the prairie near Walnut Grove, Minnesota, in the late 1800s and early 1900s. This show was based on the series of *Little House on the Prairie* books written by Laura Ingalls Wilder. The Ingalls family had strong Christian and family values. I enjoyed watching this show and seeing how they lived back then. It reminded me of how I liked playing in the bunkhouse at my grandparents' house as a kid and pretending it was a different time. I don't think I would've been able to live without some of our modern conveniences that make our lives easier; however, along with the modern conveniences and technology, we seem to trade off some of our cherished values.

I also enjoyed watching the variety shows that were on TV with my family in the evenings. We would watch shows like *The Carol Burnett Show*, *The Sonny and Cher Show*, and *The Donny and Marie Show*. They were filled with good classic humor and wonderful dancing and singing that wasn't sexually suggestive. Today's television programming has evolved into reality TV. It seems we Americans enjoy watching others' lives instead of living our own! People like to escape their own reality and spend hours watching what the television producers *show* us is reality.

After school, I enjoyed watching *The Brady Bunch* and other family-oriented programs. *The Brady Bunch* was about the lives of a man and his three sons after he marries a woman with three daughters. They focused on solving the everyday problems that most kids have. When I watched this program, I always wanted to be Marcia, the oldest daughter. She was so pretty with her long hair, and she was very popular. She was older than I was at the time, and she was everything that I wanted to be.

One television show that was also on at this time that was pushing the envelope was *All in the Family*. This was, in large part, due to the issues they discussed. This was a show that was about a husband and wife living in Queens, New York. He was rather set in his ways and was extremely opinionated. He didn't like anything that was different from himself, especially his son-in-law and minorities. They showed and discussed issues such as women's liberation, miscarriage, rape, racism, homosexuality, and breast cancer. These were subjects that weren't normally discussed on television or in families aloud.

All these television shows can be purchased on DVD (digital video disc) now for everyone to enjoy. They are even in boxed sets that include all the episodes and complete seasons. Most libraries today have DVDs of these programs that they lend out and then there is no cost. It's too bad that more families, especially families with children in particular, don't get them and watch them together. They might remember how it was *and* how it could be again. (There will be more information on DVDs later.)

On Saturdays, I remember watching the cartoons on television in the morning. They weren't filled with violence and superheroes as today's cartoons are. One cartoon that has a funny story attached to it is *The Bullwinkle Show*. This was about a moose and a chipmunk who were friends and showed the escapades they got into. At the beginning of the cartoon during the introduction, the moose, Bullwinkle, is dressed up as a magician. He is going to pull a rabbit out of a hat, and he says, "Nothin' up my sleeve!" However, both my husband and I as kids always thought he said, "Puffin' up my sleeve!" since he pulled up his sleeve while saying this. Then he reaches into the hat and pulls out a lion's head instead. What intrigued me so much was that both of us, growing up in separate households, in separate towns, always thought he said the same thing. We both had the same misunderstanding until in our adult years, we were discussing this cartoon and it came out in the conversation that this is what we thought he said, and my sister set us straight. I think we laughed for about two full minutes over that with my sister looking on in bewilderment.

Comic books have changed immensely too right along with the cartoons. I loved reading the *Archie Comics* comic books. These were based around Archie, Jughead, Veronica, Betty, and others who were attending Riverdale High School. They showed lighthearted humor, some romance situations, and mild slapstick and violence (like THUD and WHACK). Archie *really* liked Veronica, Betty *really* liked Archie, and it was interesting to see how each section in the comic book would end. Usually the good guy came out ahead. The comic books today are mostly about evil people with powers trying to destroy someone or something else.

Television broadcasting used to end with a signal when the programming was finished; after that, all that showed on the screen was a series of colored lines and there would be an annoying continuous beep. Today, however, there is never any downtime since there is something being broadcast *all* the time.

I mentioned earlier in the preface that the TVs had dials. These turned either direction and allowed for the TV channel to be changed. Inevitably, the dial would eventually break off and need to be placed back on. Over time, this wouldn't work too well, so most TVs had the proverbial pliers sitting on top of them so that they could be used at a moment's notice.

There were no remote controls either. *My sister and I* became the remotes! We changed the channels for our dad when he didn't want to get up to do it. (I know I probably would've done the same thing if I hadn't had a remote when my children were younger.)

Televisions have come a long way too. I remember having a color TV, but we were fortunate since some of my friends and other people still only had black-and-white TVs. Now, however, there is much more than just a *color* TV to enjoy. There are big-screen, flat-screen, or LED (light-emitting diode), LCD (liquid crystal display), and now HD (high-definition) TVs. A new live mobile TV is now on the market. They are calling it the FLO TV. This is for those who want to watch something on the go. From what I'm hearing, 3-D TVs are just becoming available, and I'm sure that they will become wildly popular.

Drive-in movie theaters were popular when I was a kid. They showed the big-screen movies, and people would load up the family and drive to the theater. What a treat it was. My sister and I would sit in the backseat and get to have popcorn while watching the movie. The sound came through a speaker that was attached to the car window. We would try as hard as we could to stay awake, but most of the time, I know I fell asleep.

As a teenager, the town next to where we lived, Plentywood, Montana, had one drive-in movie theater. This is that theater as it looks today. It

was a wonderful way to keep the teenagers busy during the summer. In Montana, there are only a few drive-in movie theaters still open. Here are some pictures of a couple that I found. (Another humorous point about the name of that town, Plentywood, is that my dad sometimes referred to it as Many Sticks.)

Going to the movie theater was fun too. In the summer, we would buy summer passes and get to go every week, sometimes even twice. The treats were great too. We would get to buy popcorn and a soda on most occasions. Today going to the movies at the theater costs an arm and a leg and *then* your other arm and leg if you choose to purchase any treats since you are not permitted to bring in your own items.

Movie theaters were the only way to watch movies until the VCR (videocassette recorder) was invented. The movies from my childhood were lacking the special effects of today that are standard however. I remember the movie *Jaws* and how it was *so* scary. The outer space movies seemed very cool at the time too. (As a side note, it is intriguing to me that this word *cool* has survived as popular slang for so long!) When my children watch a movie that was made in the early 1970s up through the 1980s, all they can do is make fun of the whole thing. Granted, I even watch them and think that they are rather hokey, but back then, they were great.

We also didn't have VCRs (videocassette recorders) for quite some time. The first ones to become available were beta machines, which is a type of a videocassette tape format. Then the VCR with VHS, which is another type of a videocassette tape format, became available. People that didn't own their own beta machine or VCR could rent them from stores that rented videos. It was always interesting to rent the machine and come home and *try* to hook it up properly so that you could watch the videos that you rented. Most of the time it took us longer than we liked to figure it out, and there went some of our movie time.

Today we still have the VCR with the VHS tapes, but now there is the DVD, an optical disc that can store a large amount of digital data as text, music, or images. Another player available to watch movies on DVD is the Blu-ray player. There are fewer stores today that rent videos and DVDs than there used to be; however, now a person can rent DVDs at locations that have redboxes. These are computer-operated redboxes, hence the name

I'm guessing. Anyone can use a debit or credit card to purchase one night's rental. The cost is reasonable, and if the DVD isn't returned the next day, they just charge your card again. They will do this for up to twenty days if the DVD isn't returned. By this time, the company has made their money on the DVD, and they say it is "yours." This is so handy and can be used by anyone with the correct payment type. Any rental can be returned at *any* redbox location, which makes it even *more* convenient.

When my children were still at home, we purchased the *Little House on the Prairie* DVDs. There were a total of ten seasons, and my family truly enjoyed watching these episodes together. Now that my children are living out on their own, my husband and I still like watching these since there isn't too much on television that is as wholesome and that we both enjoy.

As with most good things, there are always a couple of bad things that seem to happen. With all these advances in how a person can watch movies today, there are some people who have discovered a way to pirate the movies. They use their computers to copy them. Then they have the movies without purchasing them from the store. Some people have even made this a business and sell these pirated movies illegally. Apparently, it is a huge business for some.

In most homes that have satellite and/or cable TV, they have the option to purchase a DVR (digital video recorder). This machine records from the satellite to itself *without* videotapes. It also allows a person to skip through the commercials and then get back to live TV. I'm sure the advertisers don't appreciate this new feature very much, but the consumers sure do. We've definitely come a long way in our capability to watch TV and to record movies.

Everyone knows that sex sells, and that is exactly what *everything* has in it. Then they throw in some violence along with some bad language, and it's a huge hit. This is too bad, but it really illustrates again what is happening to our society as a whole.

Music was much more understandable and not so filled with violence, bad language, and bad behavior. Granted, each generation has issues with their children's tastes in music. For my parent's generation, Elvis Presley was a very popular artist, and most adults didn't like their kids listening to his music. For my generation, my parents didn't like the music my sister and I listened to. It is the same today as it was then. I, along with a lot of other parents, don't like most of the music my children listen to. It seems to have gotten worse with time though. Who knows what the music will sound like for the generations to come?

Music, when I was a kid, was listened to on the radio; and if you were one of the fortunate kids, you had your own portable record player or phonograph. These were small machines that looked like a small suitcase and inside there was a place to put the record. Some  homes had a large record player or phonograph that was inside a piece of furniture, complete with the speakers and space to store some records.

A record was a grooved round vinyl disc with a hole in the middle. The record would stay in the right position for the record player's arm and needle to then play the music. These record players could play 45s, 33s,

and 78s. The number indicated how many revolutions per minute there was. These record albums, or LPs (long-playing record), as they were called are fairly nonexistent today. I've heard that some Generation Yers have seen these LPs either in their grandparent's houses or at garage sales and thought they were Frisbees.

Jukeboxes are slowly becoming extinct also. These are machines that play the 45 records mentioned earlier. They cost twenty-five cents and that would play a few songs. A few restaurants would have smaller versions at their tables. I remember a restaurant in Billings, Montana, that had phones along the side of a small jukebox on the table that played the music.

An individual would place their order on the phone and then they could put some coins in and choose what music they wanted to listen to.

From there we had the 8-track players. These were machines the

size of a small stereo that played the rectangular plastic 8-tracks. They had eight tracks or songs on them, hence the name. Then we had the

cassette tape. These allowed for smaller tapes and more songs on each one. These cassettes had two sides—an A and a B side. Most cars had at least an 8-track player or a cassette player in them by the time I was a teenager. If the car had one or the other, a person could buy a converter to play whichever you wanted.

From there the CD (compact disc) was invented, and there are sound files available everywhere. As with everything that improves and changes, the sound quality greatly improved with every new way to listen to music. As mentioned before, some people have figured out ways to pirate music and, therefore, not purchase the CDs in the stores, similar to the pirating of movies.

Additional ways to listen to music currently is to download songs that are purchased from the Internet through third-party software companies. These songs can be downloaded to a DAP (digital audio player), which is a device that stores, organizes, and plays audio files. Two types of these digital audio players are the MP3 player and the iPod. The music can also be downloaded onto a computer. This allows a person to be able to choose any genre of music and not have to purchase each individual album.

The capability to record home movies has come a long way also. When I was growing up, I remember the bright light that accompanied being recorded. These were only black-and-white, with no sound, and were on big reels similar to what you see the movie theaters using. The camcorders that followed in 1983 were much smaller and had sound and color. They were still like carrying a VCR on your shoulder, however. Today we are grateful for digital devices since our home movies can also be transferred to DVDs.

It is interesting to me how everything invented seems to have initials for it. We've created acronyms for almost everything. It's almost as if we are incapable of saying the whole name or just lazy and have to shorten it for convenience.

Filming with a still camera has evolved into smaller and better quality as well. As a child, I had a camera that used 110 film and needed a separate flash to take pictures indoors. These would have the capability to take twelve or twenty-four photos. I also remember Polaroid cameras. These were one of the first brands of instant cameras. These cameras enabled a person to take a picture, and it would come out of the camera instantly. The picture would then have to develop. This took approximately two to three minutes to completely be finished. It was very interesting to me to watch it and see what the picture looked like as it was finishing developing. We always had to be careful not to touch the surface of the picture as it was developing since this could make the picture smear.

The next camera that I had was a 35 millimeter (mm) camera. The flash was built-in and took much better quality pictures. Then digital was invented, and now we don't have to have negatives of our pictures, we can keep them on a memory card, print them, or put them on a disc or in a computer. The software for today's cameras allows a person to fix red-eye, glare, and so much more.

Video games have also changed from when I was a kid. Some kids had the Atari, which was a game like tennis or ping-pong that played on the television through a console. It was a slow-moving game that was controlled by turning a knob on the controller. This advanced to the video games that were located in the arcades. Some that I can remember from my generation are PacMan, Donkey Kong, Centipede, and Asteroids. The next systems or consoles that were the rage for kids of the next generation to play were Nintendo, Super Nintendo, Game Boy, PlayStation, Xbox 360, Wii, and I'm sure many more.

My Own Recollections

(6)

Remember When . . .
Technology Was Easier to Keep Up with

Remember when technology was easier to keep up with? I certainly do. Growing up we had a few new items to have to learn to use, but not like today. The pocket calculator was a wonderful invention in 1971. Although in school, we weren't allowed to use them. These days the kids can use calculators, scientific calculators, and whatever else they have to help them, even during tests or exams.

Technology seems to always be improving. This keeps the consumer on their toes if they want to stay up-to-date on everything. These days it seems like there is something new almost monthly. Cell phones, digital cameras, computers, and most electronic products seem to be old and outdated shortly after being purchased. I need to hurry and finish this book before too many more new and updated things are invented. I'm sure there are things that I have missed though, and I apologize.

Medical technological advances have greatly improved too. I wore glasses from the third grade on, and needless to say, I had to go to the eye doctor every year so that I could see the board in school. These visits *always* led to needing stronger lenses in my glasses. I always prayed that my eyes would get better and not worse so that I could get lenses that weren't as strong and then they wouldn't have to be so thick. There weren't too many good styles for thick lenses in the 1970s and 1980s. A favorite name that kids called other kids with glasses was "Four Eyes," and I didn't like being called names. Unfortunately, some kids are still doing this.

What a blessing it was for me when the rolled and polished lenses and polycarbonate lenses came along. These at least weren't as awful looking. I was tremendously happy when contact lenses were invented, and I was allowed to get them as a teenager.

I was enormously blessed when as an adult I took advantage of the new laser eye surgery for nearsightedness and was able to throw my glasses away completely. I didn't literally throw them away. I donated them and all my old pairs that I had to a charity that gives them to people in less fortunate countries.

I am very glad for a number of other things that were invented. One would be the curling iron. As a kid, for my mom to get my hair to curl, she would use hair rollers, or curlers. These were round tubes that were  wound around some hair and put in place with a pick. I remember Mom would want our hair to look good for special occasions, and she would sit Devi and me down one at a time, fresh from having our hair shampooed, and put these rollers and picks into our hair. It felt like she was going straight in with the picks sometimes. I'm sure she got tired of us moving around, and this could've been one way to get us to hold still. Of course, we *hated* the whole process as we had to sleep in these things. There were no hair dryers for home use at this time either, so for the rollers to do their work, the hair had to be completely dry before they came out. All this for some body and *potential* curl in my stick-straight hair.

Also as a kid, I remember for a while in the airport if you had to use the restroom, it cost ten cents. I don't know if this was just a phase to try and make some extra money for the airport or what, but it didn't last long. It seemed like I always had to use the bathroom when we went to the airport to pick someone up or send someone off. My mom would always have us crawl *under* the door. *Yuck!* Just to save ten cents! Today it doesn't cost to use the bathroom, and in some places, the toilet flushes automatically for you. Most public restrooms even have automatic faucets *and* hand dryers.

Advanced technology is good for certain things, but it does have its drawbacks. It is good to progress; however, it is bad to move away from family values and being too busy to spend time *with* your family. It would do us all good to know how things were done in the old days. I, for one, struggle when the power goes off even for a short time.

It seems like the kids of today, the Generation Yers, are always busy. Busy with computer games, video games, and their laptops. They are also *always* busy with their cell phones—texting, texting, and texting. With texting, the ability to spell properly is being compromised. (Also, I fear that they will have long-lasting damage to their thumbs!) This next generation seems to be losing its ability to hold meaningful conversations. They are communicating with each other more, but they are *saying* less. I really would like there to be more quality family time in today's families. Time that everyone is unplugged from all the electronic devices. Heaven help us all if there wasn't a way to charge all our must-have electronic devices. I think the world would come to a stop.

Banking has changed drastically from generation to generation too. Most people in my generation and those who are older still write checks and manage our bank accounts manually in a check register. We actually reconcile our bank statements monthly that come to us in the mail. The next generation, the Generation Yers, prefers the paperless online way of doing this. They use debit cards instead of paper checks, and rather than do a reconciliation monthly, they just look up their account balances on their computers when they need to know how much money they have available.

My children are now grown and on their own, but for future generations, it would be nice to have some of the olden days back. When families would be able to spend some real quality time together, other than on holidays and for weddings and funerals.

With all the advances in technology that are supposed to help us save time, I feel that we don't have *enough* time. Not enough time for the important things in life: faith, family, and friends.

My Own Recollections

(7)

Remember When . . .
Families Worked Together

Remember when families worked together? If both parents worked outside the home, most children would help out around the house when they weren't in school. Both of my parents worked outside the home, so when we were older, my sister and I would do things around the house. Every night, we would do the dishes. One would wash and the other would dry. Then we would switch duties the next night. When Devi would be washing, she always seemed to be finished *way* before me. Once I caught her washing the dishes and not putting them in the rinse water right away. Then all of a sudden, when she was almost done, she put them *all* in the rinse water, making me rinse and dry all these while she was done! Sneaky.

I hated to get dirty as a kid and honestly still do, so I didn't like yard work. However, when the grass needed mowing, we would mow it. We had a lawn mower that you would just push and the blades would rotate. This lawn mower was noisy since it was made of metal and would get rusty. With this lawn mower, the grass clippings would remain on the ground. Sometimes, we had to rake up these grass clippings. As a teenager, we finally got an electric lawn mower. Using it, I was scared that I would run over the extension cord since Mom warned us that if we did, we could be electrocuted. This lawn mower had a bag attached that would catch the grass clippings and then needs emptying when it got full. When it was full, it got very heavy. It would've been much easier to empty the bag more often, but I always seemed to wait until it was *really* full and then it was *really* heavy.

For the trimming, there were no such things as electric edgers, electric trimmers, or weed eaters. We had these handheld clippers that looked like a very big pair of sharp metal scissors. These would be used on the edge of the sidewalk, around the trees, or anywhere the lawn mower couldn't reach. My mom didn't like weeds, so she was always pulling them out (and my sister and I did too) using another tool that would remove the dandelions from the grass. This tool looked like a small version of what the pictures of the devil's fork look like. This would push into the ground, and with a yank, the dandelions would come out, hopefully with most of the root attached. In between the cracks of the sidewalk, we would have to pull those weeds too, by hand, over and over again. There was no such thing as Roundup weed killer for household use back then.

We washed the car in the summer if we were asked to. Or if it was an exceptionally hot day, *we* would *ask* to wash the car. We also got some sun, which we thought was great since getting a suntan was very important to young teenage girls in those days. This was all done by hand. There were no wands or fancy things to attach to the hose. We would just use the hose, a bucket of soapy water, and a rag. I especially didn't like to clean the inside of the car so that was *only* done when I was asked *or told* to do it.

We took out the trash, dusted the furniture, cleaned the bathroom, cleaned our bedrooms, vacuumed, swept, mopped, and did whatever else needed done.

My parents owned a variety of small businesses during the majority of my time growing up. My dad always said to us, "Like what you do, and do what you like," and he lived by that himself. Devi and I worked in their businesses beginning around the age of ten and continued until we graduated from high school and moved away. The first business was a mom-and-pop grocery store called Miles Avenue Grocery. It was located on a corner street in a neighborhood in Billings, Montana. Our house was right beside it, and there was a hallway that connected the two together. They didn't pay us, but I'm sure I ate my wages in penny candy! This is what the building looks like today.

Next came a bowling alley in Medicine Lake, Montana, called Lake Bowl. We worked after school, evenings, and weekends. When the men bowled on their league nights, my sister and I would sometimes take score for them since there were no automatic scorekeepers then. We got twenty-five cents per bowler per game. We thought that was great. Some people, bowlers included, don't even know how to keep score now because everything is done automatically for them! We also cleaned and oiled the lanes. All done by hand because the automatic ones weren't around then. We reset pins and fixed the machines if they broke down.

Since there was a small kitchen in the bowling alley, sometimes we had to cook and serve food. We bought pies from a local woman for us to sell, and they were very popular. This is what the bowling alley looks like today. This is a picture of the Brunswick machine that cleaned the balls.

We learned a lot of lessons in these businesses that our parents owned and operated. Public relations was a very important lesson we took away from helping out. Waiting on the customers taught us how to be fair and polite. Math was another huge lesson that was helpful to us

for the rest of our lives. There weren't cash registers with computers in them, so we had to do it the hard way—manually and by using our brains. Counting back change to a customer is rarely done today.

Granted, we didn't always enjoy doing these chores and jobs. We did them because we were part of the family and were asked to do them. We didn't get an allowance. We didn't feel entitled to anything extra. Some kids today feel entitled to everything and don't feel that they have to *do* anything for the things they need or want.

When I was younger and we lived in Billings, Montana, summertime was extra special. There was an ice-cream truck that would come around the neighborhood every couple of days. We would hear the music from the truck and ask Mom for some money for an ice-cream treat. We would be allowed a treat often because we did things around the house and deserved a treat.

When I was in grade school, I walked to and from school. I was known as a latchkey kid. This meant that both of my parents worked outside of the home, and the kids were home alone after school until one or both of the parents got home. So I needed a key to get in the house. After school was out for the day, it seemed that all the kids in the neighborhood would play at one house or another outside. In the backyard at one of our residences, we had a log cabin playhouse. This provided endless hours of entertainment for my sister and me and our friends. I remember having lemonade stands, flying kites, and going to the park in our neighborhood often.

We would also ride our bikes around, play games, go to the roller-skating rink, and just be kids. We usually stayed outside if the weather was good until our mom called us in for supper. This all happened in the summer too. We knew to be home by dark. We were never fearful of being kidnapped, stolen, or abused. I'm afraid that doesn't happen much today. There are way too many wackos and crazy people out there like predators and sick people who want to take and hurt children. I'm sure these people were around when I was growing up, but they weren't as prevalent and talked about in the press.

Our morals in this great country are steadily getting worse. An example of this is when I was in grade school, I remember walking around the lamppost in our yard that I always got to plant sweet alyssum in, and I was just repeating a curse word that I had learned from another kid. A boy from our neighborhood heard me and told me that he was going to tell my mom if I didn't stop. Well, *I* didn't stop, and *he* told my mom! I got in big trouble. That probably wouldn't have happened today. Most people prefer to just observe and not get involved. Even when it is something that should be stopped as in this case. Families are growing apart instead of closer. It also appears that each new generation seems to feel entitled to everything *more so* than the previous generation.

My Own Recollections

(8)

Remember When . . .
Politics Weren't as Important

I remember growing up totally unaware of what was going on around me politically and in the news. That is good for younger children; however, I think as people grow from the teenage years and beyond that they should pay closer attention to the world around them.

For starters, everyone of voting age should vote in each election. However, *only* after they have done their homework and researched what every candidate stands for. Start locally, and work your way toward the national candidates. Voting has taken on a negative connotation to some. They feel that they might have to serve on jury duty or other things. Voting needs to be viewed as it was meant when it was established in our great country. It is a privilege and needs to be taken seriously. I can't stress how important it is for everyone to get involved and stay involved.

I am finally paying closer attention to the world around me. I have voted since I was eighteen years old; however, I never did my own research on the candidates. I voted along party lines on a national level. Today I am voting for those candidates that I believe will do the best job in that position for the good of our country and its citizens. We all need to be paying better attention and demanding to know as much as we can about everything. The media only tells us what they want to. There is so much more corruption today, and as Americans, we need to be aware of it.

The Generation Yer's seem to think that if something doesn't directly affect them, then they don't need to know about it or even care about it, let alone *do* anything about it. *Everything* affects *everyone*. Consequently, we all need to be diligent and learn all that we can about what is going on around us and be prepared to do the right things.

Another thing that I think would be beneficial to everyone is that every person after their formal schooling should have to take a history class or an online history course. I would have gained a lot more out of a history class as a young adult or an older adult than I did in high school.

Being a first-year Generation Xer, the United States was at peace most of my childhood since the Vietnam War ended in 1975. While I was growing up and into my early adult life, there were no wars. There was always some strife between countries, but it seemed to be under control. As a young adult, there was the Persian Gulf War, Afghanistan, Iraq, and 9/11. Today as time has progressed and I am no longer a young adult, there seems to be an ever-growing amount of strife between countries. Just in the last few decades, there have been more wars than ever before that the United States is involved in. The conflicts are growing, and the threat of terrorism is a constant danger.

I would advise everybody to stay informed and continue to pray for our country and its leaders.

My Own Recollections

(9)

Remember When . . .
Our Focus Was in the Right Order

Growing up, I remember my family's focus seemed to be in the right order. I believe that the focus should be God, family, then a person's job, and finally friends. Everything else will fall into place then: happiness, prosperity, and contentment. The morals of this great country would improve and the next generation, whatever they will be called, wouldn't feel so entitled to everything. Bigger, better, and busier seems to be the new American dream that we are striving for today. It would be wonderful to be able to do the opposite of what is the norm, and that would be to go backward instead of forward. Back to the slower and easier way of life. If we continue on the path that we are currently on, the future for us and our children and the generations to come seems very overwhelming and daunting.

I'm sure each generation has their ideas and memories of better days. For instance, my parents' generation. Growing up as teenagers in the '50s and '60s, they had the great clothes, the music, and the sock hops. And their parents, my grandparents' generation, had *their* own great memories of how wonderful life was for *them*!

Depending on what you are, a pre-baby boomer, a baby boomer, a Generation Xer, a Generation Yer, or even beyond that, I hope that you have enjoyed catching up on old times, traveling down memory lane, or found our olden days interesting while maybe even learning something.

With permission from my mom, I am including a poem that her dad, my grandfather, wrote as an adult. I found it to be very fitting for what I am trying to express throughout this book.

The Old Ways

As I sit here and daydream, my thoughts wander on,
to the Old-fashioned ways, and the days that are gone.
The old pioneer with his oxen and plow,
or the old covered wagon, you don't see them now
as rare as a prospector mucking for gold.
    You can think of the new ways
        and I'll dream of the Old.

The little log cabin, with dirt for a floor,
and the leather latch string that hung from the door.
The old flintlock rifle that hung on the wall,
and the horn, when the children came home at its call
to the old fireplace when the evenings were cold.
    You can think of the new ways
        while I dream of the Old.

So I sit here and dream as time wanders on,
of the old pioneers and the days that are gone.
They are ashes of memories blown into the past,
and their dust on the prairies has settled at last
on their trails that they blazed on their wandering through.
    I'll still dream of the old days
        while I live in the new.
           (Bob Evans)

My Own Recollections

Index

Internet, 18, 21-23, 63
iPad, 23
iPod, 63

J

Jaws, 60
Jetsons, The, 22
Jiffy Pop Popcorn, 31
Jukeboxes, 62

K

Kindle, 23
Kmart, 27

L

Lake Bowl, 74
laptop, 23
laser eye surgery, 68
latchkey kid, 75
lawn mowing, 72
license plate game, 44
Little House on the Prairie (Ingalls
    Wilder), 57, 61
long-playing record (LP), 62

M

manual typewriter, 19-20
marijuana, 51
Mayberry, North Carolina, 56
McDonald's, 27
measles, 53
memory stick, 23
meth, 51
methicillin-resistant *Staphylococcus
    aureus* (MRSA), 53

microwave oven, 9, 28
microwave popcorn, 31-32
Miles Avenue Grocery, 73
Milwaukee, Wisconsin, 56
Monopoly, 37
Montana
    Billings, 27-28, 39, 62, 73, 75
    Fort Smith, 38
    Glendive, 39-40, 47
    Medicine Lake, 15, 19, 28, 40, 74
    Plentywood, 59
    Wibaux, 41, 45, 47
morals, 75, 82
MP3 player, 63
mumps, 53
music, 18, 56, 60-63, 75, 82
MySpace, 24

N

nicknames, 37
Nintendo, 23, 64
Nintendo DS, 23
Nook, 23

O

"Old Ways, The" (Evans), 83

P

PacMan, 64
PalmPilot, 23
party lines, 16, 78
pay phones, 16-17
Persian Gulf War, 79
personal computer (PC), 20, 23
personal digital assistant (PDA), 18
phone

bag, 18
cordless, 17
push-button, 16-17
rotary dial, 15, 16
phone booths, 16
phonograph, 62
piracy, 61, 63
PlayStation, 64
pocket calculator, 67
Polaroid cameras, 64
polio, 53
popcorn, 29, 31-32, 59-60
portable record player, 62
pre-baby boomers, 9, 19, 82
pregnancy, 52
premarital sex, 52
prepackaged foods, 27-28
prescription drugs, 51
Presley, Elvis, 18, 61

Q

Queens, New York, 57

R

radar detector, 38
records, 18, 20, 61-63
Recycling, 29-30
redboxes, 60
rubella, 53

S

scientific calculators, 67
seat belts, 46
severe acute respiratory syndrome (SARS), 53
sex, 52, 56, 61

sexually transmitted disease, 52
shorthand, 20
"Sixteen Tons" (Ford), 44
smallpox, 53
Snack Pack pudding, 28
snail mail, 21, 24
social networking sites (SNS), 24
Sonny and Cher Show, The, 57
Sorry, 37
Star Wars, 30
Super Nintendo, 64
swine flu, 53

T

Tasty Hut, 42
television
big-screen, 59
black-and-white, 59
color, 59
flat-screen, 59
high-definition (HD), 59
light-emitting diode (LED), 59
liquid crystal display (LCD), 59
3-D, 59
texting, 16, 69
35 millimeter (mm) camera, 64
"This Land Is Your Land," 44
toaster ovens, 28
TV dinners, 28
Twitter, 24
typing, 19-20

V

vending machines, 29
VHS, 60
videocassette recorder (VCR), 60, 64
video games, 64, 69

Edwards Brothers,Incl
Thorofare, NJ 08086
18 November, 2010
BA2010323